A NOTE TO PARENTS

When your children are ready to "step into reading," giving them the right books—and lots of them—is as crucial as giving them the right food to eat. **Step into Reading Books** present exciting stories and information reinforced with lively, colorful illustrations that make learning to read fun, satisfying, and worthwhile. They are priced so that acquiring an entire library of them is affordable. And they are beginning readers with an important difference—they're written on four levels.

Step 1 Books, with their very large type and extremely simple vocabulary, have been created for the very youngest readers. **Step 2 Books** are both longer and slightly more difficult. **Step 3 Books,** written to mid-second-grade reading levels, are for the child who has acquired even greater reading skills. **Step 4 Books** offer exciting nonfiction for the increasingly proficient reader.

Children develop at different ages. **Step into Reading Books,** with their four levels of reading, are designed to help children become good—and interested—readers *faster*. The grade levels assigned to the four steps—preschool through grade 1 for Step 1, grades 1 through 3 for Step 2, grades 2 and 3 for Step 3, and grades 2 through 4 for Step 4—are intended only as guides. Some children move through all four steps very rapidly; others climb the steps over a period of several years. These books will help your child "step into reading" in style'

D1444837

Library of Congress Cataloging in Publication Data:
Lorian, Nicole. A birthday present for Mama. (Step into reading. A Step 2 book) SUMMARY: After considering many possibilities, Little Rabbit inadvertently gives his mother a very special birthday present. [1. Birthdays–Fiction. 2. Gifts–Fiction. 3. Rabbits–Fiction] I. Miller, J.P. (John Parr), 1913– , ill. II. Title. III. Series. PZ7.L8865Bi 1984 [E] 83-26849 ISBN: 0-394-86755-6 (trade); 0-394-96755-0 (lib. bdg.)

Manufactured in the United States of America 13 14 15 16 17 18 19 20

Step into Reading™

A Birthday Present for Mama

by Nicole Lorian
illustrated by J. P. Miller

A Step 2 Book

Random House 🏠 New York

One morning Little Rabbit
woke up very early.
"Today is Mama's birthday
and I have nothing
to give her,"
he said.

Little Rabbit jumped out of bed

and shook his bunny bank.

Out came two big silver coins . . .

and many little brown coins.

"What a lot of money!

I can buy her

a wonderful present

in town," he said.

He got dressed.

But he did not wash

his face or ears.

He did not eat breakfast.

Little Rabbit was in a hurry!

Little Rabbit went very quietly

past Mama Rabbit's room

and out of the house.

He ran across Sheep Meadow.

"Good morning, Little Lamb.

I am off to buy

a wonderful present for Mama!"

he said.

"A gold ring . . .

or a pearl necklace . . .

or maybe a silver watch."

"Why not give her
a warm wool coat?"
asked Little Lamb.

"No," said Little Rabbit.

"My mama has a warm fur coat."

Then he went through the gate
and onto the road to town.

Little Rabbit went right to
Jack's Super Store.

"I am looking for

  a birthday present for Mama,"

he said to Mr. Jack.

"Do you have a gold ring?

  Or a pearl necklace?

  Or a silver watch?"

He put his money on the counter.

"I am sorry, Little Rabbit,

but you need a lot more money

for a gold ring

or a pearl necklace

or a silver watch,"

said Mr. Jack.

He held up an apron.

"You can buy her this nice apron."

Little Rabbit shook his head.

"Mama has an apron."

Little Rabbit looked

all around the store.

He saw many things.

Then he saw something wonderful!

It was a little toy car.

He ran the car

up the counter

and down the counter.

"I will take it!"

said Little Rabbit happily.

Mr. Jack looked surprised.

"A TOY for your mama?"

asked Mr. Jack.

"Well," said Little Rabbit,

"maybe a toy is not

the right present for Mama.

But what CAN I give her?"

Mr. Jack smiled.

"Cheer up, Little Rabbit.

You will think of something,"

he said.

"I will ask my friends
to help me,"
said Little Rabbit.
He waved good-bye to Mr. Jack.

Then he went to the town pond.

"Little Frog," he said,

"today is Mama's birthday.

What should I give her?"

"A fly!" said Little Frog.

"A big black fly.

That is what I would give

my mama."

Just then a big black fly

flew by.

Little Frog opened his mouth.

"Hmmm, good!" said Little Frog.

Little Rabbit said,

"Not so good for my mama!"

And off he went.

"Oh, what IS a nice

little surprise for Mama?"

he wondered.

Little Rabbit asked his friend
Little Dog.
"Give her a bone!"
said Little Dog.

Then Little Rabbit asked

his friend Little Cat.

"Give her a fish!"

said Little Cat.

"No, thanks!" said Little Rabbit
  to the dog and the cat.
"I will ask my friends
  in the woods."
  There he saw
  Little Bird and Little Squirrel.
"I need a present for Mama.
  Can you help me?"
  he asked them.

"Give her a big fat worm!"
said Little Bird.

"No!" said Little Squirrel.

"I know something that is
little but nice.
Nuts! Give her nuts!"

Little Rabbit wanted to say
"Nuts to that!"
But he just said, "No, thanks!"
Then he went deep into the woods.

Suddenly a red animal
with a big bushy tail
jumped out of a bush
and shouted, "Boo!"

Little Rabbit jumped.

The red animal laughed.

"Do you want to play with me?

I am Little Fox.

Who are you?"

Little Rabbit said,

"I am Little Rabbit."

The fox licked his lips.

"Oh, so you are a little rabbit!

I am so happy to meet you.

But what brings you here?"

asked the fox.

"I am looking for a present for my mama.

Today is her birthday

and I do not know

what to give her,"

said Little Rabbit.

The fox laughed and laughed.

"What is so funny?"

asked Little Rabbit.

"Today is MY mama's birthday too,"

said the fox.

"But I know what

I am going to give her. . .

. . . a fat little rabbit!"

Then the fox jumped

at Little Rabbit.

This time he did not say "Boo!"

But Little Rabbit was quick.

He ran over logs,

around trees,

and across the stream.

The fox ran after him.

Little Rabbit ran
out of the woods.
He squeezed through
a farmer's fence.

The fox stopped at the fence.

He was too big

to squeeze through it.

Little Rabbit was safe!

But Little Rabbit was very tired.

And still he did not know

what to give his mama.

Not a coat . . .

or an apron . . .

or a toy.

Not a fly . . .

or a bone . . .

or a fish . . .

or a worm . . .

or a nut.

And he was hungry, too.

He ate a carrot.

"Hmmm, good!" he said.

And then he knew

what to give his mama.

"Carrots! Mama loves carrots!"

But just then a man yelled,

"Get out of my garden!"

The man ran after him.

Little Rabbit dropped the carrots

and ran to the fence.

He was so scared

that he ran all the way home.

Oh, was he happy to see

his mama in the doorway!

He ran right into her arms
and gave her a big hug.
"Why, thank you, Little Rabbit,"
said his mama.
"How did you know
that a big hug from you
was just the birthday surprise
I wanted!"
Then Little Rabbit's mama
gave him a big hug.

That night Little Rabbit
went to bed very tired
but very happy.